My First Monologue Book

SMITH AND KRAUS

Young Actors Series for Grades K–6

MONOLOGUES AND SCENES

Cool Characters for Kids Volume I: 71 One-Minute Monologues MILSTEIN isbn 1-57525-
306-2 $11.95 pages: 78

Great Scenes and Monologues For Children ages 7–14 Volumes I and II

Wild and Wacky! 61 One-Minute Monologues for Kids Volume I

PLAYS

10-Minute Plays Volume IV for Kids/10+ Format* Comedy by KRISTEN DABROWSKI

10-Minute Plays Volume V for Kids/10+ Format* Drama by KRISTEN DABROWSKI

Multicultural Plays for Children Grades K–3 by PAMELA GERKE

Multicultural Plays for Children Grades 4–6 by PAMELA GERKE

Fairy Tales, Grades K–3 by MCCULLOUGH

Mythology, Grades 4–6 by L. E. MCCULLOUGH

People at Work, Grades K–3 by L. E. MCCULLOUGH

Now I Get It!" Grades K–3 36 Ten-Minute Skits about Science, Math, Language, and
Social Studies for Fun and Learning by L. E. MCCULLOUGH

Now I Get It!" Grades 4–6 36 Ten-Minute Skits about Science, Math, Language, and
Social Studies for Fun and Learning by L. E. MCCULLOUGH

Ancient Israel, Grades K–3 by L. E. MCCULLOUGH

Israel Reborn, Grades 4–6 by L. E. MCCULLOUGH

Plays of the Songs of Christmas by L. E. MCCULLOUGH

America from American Folklore, Grades K–6 by L. E. MCCULLOUGH

Wild West, Grades K–3 by L. E. MCCULLOUGH

Wild West, Grades 4–6 by L. E. MCCULLOUGH

Exploration and Discovery, Grades 4–6 by L. E. MCCULLOUGH

To receive prepublication information about upcoming Smith and Kraus books and information
about special promotions, send us your e-mail address at info@smithandkraus.com with a
subject line of MAILING LIST. You may receive our annual catalogue, free of charge, by send-
ing your name and address to *Smith and Kraus Catalogue, PO Box 127, Lyme, NH 03768.
Call us at (888) 282-2881; fax (603) 643-1831 or visit us at SmithandKraus.com.*

My First Monologue Book

100 Monologues for Young Children

by Kristen Dabrowski

YOUNG ACTORS SERIES

A SMITH AND KRAUS BOOK

A Smith and Kraus Book
Published by Smith and Kraus, Inc.
177 Lyme Road, Hanover, NH 03755
www.SmithandKraus.com

First Edition: November 2006
Manufactured in the United States of America
9 8 7 6 5 4 3 2 1

Cover and text design by Julia Gignoux, Freedom Hill Design

ISBN 1-57525-533-2
Library of Congress Control Number: 2006938162

*To Mary Hyer for being so much fun and
to Helen Payne for always being kind.*

*Plus, special thanks to Addy, Weezie, Gerry,
Gordon, and Cat for their stories.
You kids are weird!*

Contents

Foreword

FOR KIDS

Hello, young actors! Monologue is a big, strange word. But the meaning is simple—it's one person doing a lot of talking. So monologues are fun for actors to do! You can really show off and have a good time imagining you are a lot of different people.

These monologues are for kids only! Many of the monologues are true stories from my life and from my friends' lives. People your age have read them and like them. Hopefully, you will, too.

To be really, really good, it helps to practice saying the monologue you choose a bunch of times. Try saying it with different voices, when you're in different moods, and in different places. Imagine where you are and what your character likes and wears. Dress up for it!

You can practice and perform these monologues for your parents, friends, and even for showbiz people. Feel free to ask your parents for help with any words that you don't understand. Have fun!

FOR PARENTS, TEACHERS, AND AGENTS

These monologues are about kids and for kids. Often, kids are given material meant for adults or adult actors. This is hard for them to read and act. *This book contains situations kids can relate to and understand.* Some of the words may be challenging on the page, but they are easily understood.

Inside, you'll see a great variety of scenarios and emotions to choose from. Often, the monologues change mood or direction so the actor can show a range. They are kept short and sweet so they don't overwhelm. A few are particularly brief, though specific and finely tuned, for early readers.

There are a lot of character types that kids recognize from their lives—the show-off, the chicken, the boss, the teacher's pet, etc. Encouraging them to really play up the feelings and character types often has dramatic results. I have often seen shy children transform into big hams!

If you'd like, change a girl's speech to a boy's speech or vice versa. If you need or want to change a word, do it! You can do anything you want with these monologues. Teachers, these monologues may spark the imaginations of your students. See if they can write their own.

The topics and language are kid-tested and approved from my work in New York schools and summer camps. Enjoy and explore!

Kristen Dabrowski

FUN AND GAMES

Games are fun!
(Sometimes . . .)

JOE

Joe just finished playing a board game with his family. He lost.

I hate losing! You cheated! This game is stupid. I don't care if I broke the game board.

I don't see why *she's* crying; *I'm* the one who lost this stupid game. You have no reason to be upset! I'm never, ever playing this game again!

Don't worry. I'm already going to my room. It's better than being here.

MICHELLE

Michelle likes to play house with her best friend, Ana. But Ana doesn't want to play house any more.

Let's play house. I'll be the mom, and you can be the baby. How come you don't want to play? We can find someone else to be the baby, if you want.

We're not too old to play this game. It's not baby stuff! We could play school instead, and I could be the teacher— Well, what do *you* want to play, Ana?

You want to stand around staring at each other? Why? Your sister does that with her friends? I'm never going to be a teenager. It sounds boring!

JULIA

Julia likes to play tag with the boys. But they always make her "it." Julia's not very fast, so she's "it" a lot!

Why am I always *it*? I'm sick of it. Why don't you be *it* first, Brian? Just this time? Please? Why not? I thought you were my friend. You won't be my friend unless I'm *it* first? I just don't want to be *it* this one little time! Please?

(Shouting.) Mr. Sipp, Brian won't be *it*!

I have to tell on you. You're being mean.

You'll be *it*? Really? Really really?

Wait! You can't tag me that fast. You guys? Wait up!

NICK

Nick is playing tag. He just tagged his friend, Ross.

I tagged you. I did! I got your shirt. I did, too! You just don't want to be *it*. You always pretend you didn't feel it. It's not how you play the game. You have to be *it* sometimes. You can't always get your way. It's part of the game. You're *it*! Come on! You *have* to! Stop being such a baby. You're no fun to play with. Know what, I'm not playing anymore. And I won't play ever again unless you learn to play right. That means you're *(Tagging imaginary person in front of him.)* IT!

OPAL

Opal wants to play tag, but no one wants to play with her. When she's "it," she chases after the same boy every time!

Why won't anybody tag me? I *do* play the game right. I don't cheat! When you're *it*, you can tag whoever you want. If I only want to tag Travis, I can do that! That's in the rules. I *like* to tag Travis. I don't want to marry him! Ew! Quit it!

Come *on*, somebody tag me! I want to be *it*! I'm standing right here. I'm not even moving. Come on!

TARA

Tara is telling her mom that she doesn't want to go to ballet class any more.

I hate ballet class. How come we have to repeat the same things every week? I was good the first time. I don't get why we have to do it again!

To get better? But I told you; I was good. So maybe the other kids should do it again, but I could do something new. And I want a costume! How come I have to wait? This doesn't make sense. Are you sure this teacher knows what she's doing?

DAVE

Dave is in-line skating on the sidewalk with his dad.

My teeth hurt. How come we have to skate on the sidewalk? It's too bumpy. There are hardly ever any cars around. Can I Rollerblade in the street, Dad?

What if I get killed tripping on a huge crack in the sidewalk? Plus, if you step on a crack, you break your mother's back. So if I fall down, I'll kill me *and* Mom. What do you mean, take my skates off? I'm having fun!

KEVIN

Kevin is playing with his friend, Carlos.
Carlos keeps changing the rules to the game.

I don't want to play this game any more. It's not
fun. When do I get to win? I already zapped you
twice. If my ray gun doesn't work on you, how can I
win? I hate this game. I'm going inside.

I'll stay if I can use *your* ray gun. That one works,
right? If nothing can zap you, then you always win!

OK, so if you touch the wall and you have only one
foot on the ground, and *then* I zap you, I'll win?
OK, let's go!

TONI

In gym class, the other kids want to play dodgeball. Toni hates dodgeball. She wants to play something else.

No, you guys! No! You don't know what you're saying! Dodgeball? I hate dodgeball. Scooters! We have to ask to play on the scooters. *That's* fun. Dodgeball hurts. It stings when someone hits you hard. And it's not very nice. Kids pick on other kids in dodgeball! Remember how a bunch of kids hit Amy at the same time and made her cry? That's mean.

Let's tell the teacher we want to play scooters. It doesn't hurt, unless someone runs over your hand, and it's way more fun. How come no one is listening to me? You really like dodgeball? That is so weird!

JAMES

James just skinned his knees very badly, but he wants to go back and play. He's talking to his teacher.

It doesn't hurt. I'm fine. I don't need to go to the nurse. It's not bleeding much. Can I go back and play? My mom doesn't care about my socks. I can get blood on them. It's OK.

Can I go play now? It doesn't hurt at all. See? I can touch it. I don't feel a thing. I get hurt all the time. Do I *have* to get a Band-Aid? I get dirt in my cuts all the time. My mom doesn't care. So can I go play now? The game is starting!

ABE

Abe's dad is trying to teach him to play base-ball on a hot summer day.

Dad, I'm sick of this. The mosquitoes are eating me alive. Can't we go inside now? I don't really *have* to learn to play baseball. It's OK. I think I get it now. Eyes on the ball. Right.

Maybe I'm just not any good at this. Maybe I never will be. But a guy can only be hit in the head with a baseball so many times. I'm kinda sick of this game. I don't think I want to play any more. I'll just quit the team. Can't I just quit, Dad?

GABBY

Gabby's Cousin Robbie is not a nice boy.
Gabby is telling her mom why she doesn't
want to go to cousin Robbie's house.

I hate going to Cousin Robbie's house. That Robbie is a bad boy. I hate playing with him. He always throws sand in my eyes and makes me cry. And then I have to wear Aunt Helen's big sunglasses. They make everything look pink.

Do we have to go? It hurts to have sand in your eyes, Mommy. Maybe we could just have the doughnuts instead! Aunt Helen could come if she wants. But she needs to leave that bad boy at home.

CARTER

Carter's friends won't let them in their tree house.

Hey, guys, it's me! Let me in! Why not? Come on, guys. What did I do? I *had* to bring a girl to the tree house yesterday. She's not even a girl. She's my *sister*. My mom made me take her. I couldn't help it. I would have been in big trouble if I didn't do it. I promise I'll never do it again, OK? Now I know the rules—no girls. Come on, guys! Let me in! Look, I brought some comic books. I'll let you read them if you let me—

Hey, thanks! I promise I'll never let me sister in here again. Just don't lock me out again, OK?

HARRY

Harry's friend just broke a neighbor's window while playing baseball.

Uh, oh. You're in trouble. I'm going home. No, you can't run! You have to stay and tell the lady what you did. *You* broke the window, not *me*! I'm not staying. No way! You're going to have to be the old lady's personal slave or something to pay for it. Well, you don't have money, right? Do you want her to tell your mom and dad? You'd better start crying. Maybe she'll feel sorry for you.

I did not throw the ball too hard! You *hit* the ball too hard. It's *your* fault. I'm getting out of here. Sorry, but my dad will kill me if I get in trouble! Bye! See you tomorrow!

BEAN

Bean is playing hide and seek with a bunch of boys. She can't find anybody.

Hey, where did everybody go? I give up! I counted to a hundred, like you said. It took a really long time. Where is everybody? I said I give up! I can't find you! I've been looking for ages. Can anybody hear me? This isn't funny any more, you guys. Come out, come out, wherever you are! Come on, guys.

Let's play a different game! We could play tag outside. Or maybe we could have a snack and play video games. I'll let you guys play first! I promise! Just come out. I can't find you, OK? I give up. What more do you want from me? Guys? Hey, guys?

JAKE

Jake's mom doesn't like him to play cowboys and Indians. She doesn't like shooting and fighting even if it's pretend.

Mom? I don't get this game. How come when we play cowboys and Indians we have to get along? It's not any fun when we can't shoot each other. That's the whole point of cowboys and Indians. Maybe it's not nice, but it's *fun*. We're not *really* shooting each other; we're just playing. So how is that bad? I don't want to call him a "Native American," Mom; I want to call him an Indian.

Aw, forget it, Austin. Let's just both be cowboys. We'll build a fort and pretend we see Indians. Sorry, Mom, Native Americans. Let's go outside so we can shoot Indians in peace and quiet, Austin.

I Wish, I Want

Hopes, dreams, wishes, wants,
and very tall tales!

CARA

Cara loves animals and wants to be a princess. She's talking to her mom.

If I were a princess, I'd have lots of horses and a pig called Bingo. We'd be best friends and live in a really big castle. Bingo can talk, so he'd give really good advice to the whole kingdom. Everyone would tell him their problems. Except for me. I wouldn't have any problems. Except sometimes maybe my crown might get bent when I'm riding my horses, so I could tell Bingo about that. Mom, could we please, please get a pet piggy? Who knows? We might even find a magic one who could help you with all of your problems. Please?

CHRISTINA

*Christina is a movie star. She has to stay
inside a lot by herself.*

I don't like being famous. I don't like staying inside
all day so no one can take pictures of me. I want to
go ice-skating, then go to the mall and the movies. I
want to be around other kids! It's no fun playing
with grown-ups all the time. I'm faster than you.
And you *always* let me win at board games. I can't
always win.

Can I pretend to be a regular old kid for just today?
I could put on a disguise, so no one will know it's
me. Who knows? Maybe I will even make a friend! I
just want to be a regular old kid today!

ALICIA

Alicia is a princess who doesn't like boys. She is talking to her father, the king.

Daddy, I don't want to be a princess anymore. I like the pretty dresses and I sort of like the dancing, but . . . why do I have to dance with boys? I really don't like boys. The last boy I danced with told me about all the worms he ate. How he'd get his servants to search far and wide for the fattest, juiciest worms in the kingdom. I almost puked on my pretty slippers, Daddy! It was gross.

I could just dance by myself from now on. And you, of course, because you're my dad and not a boy. But I just cannot stand another day of dancing with worm-eaters!

ANDREW

Andrew really, really likes himself. He has a
TV show. Today, his friend, Josh, is a guest
on the show.

Good morning and welcome to my TV show. Today, I will talk about how wonderful I am. I know that I talked about that yesterday, but we ran out of time, and I didn't finish. So this is Part Two. I, Andrew, am wonderful. I'm terrific. My mom tells me so. I am great at making noises. Except don't make the sound of an ambulance in the car or your mom will get mad. Here are some other things I can do: throw a baseball, hold my breath underwater for a long time, cross my eyes, tell knock-knock jokes, and run really fast.

You cannot run faster, Josh! You cannot! You're supposed to be quiet anyway! This is my show! You ruined everything! Get your own show!

GRETA

Greta wants a pony. She is asking her dad to buy her one.

How come kids in books get ponies, but I can't have one? I've never even seen a pony up close, and that is so unfair. They are just the prettiest animals possible. If I had a pony, I would brush his tail all day and night till he was so shiny it would hurt to look at him.

Why do ponies get to eat sugar cubes all day, but I can't have candy whenever I want? You don't hear about horses teeth falling out, so why would mine? I'm going to get a million dollars and then I'll buy ten thousand ponies and we'll live on a ranch in the sunshine forever and I'll ride all day.

Ponies don't smell like goats, do they? I'm sure they don't. I'm sure they smell like perfume. I can't wait till I get my pony! I just have to have one or I'll never be really, truly happy. Please, Daddy?

AUSTIN

Austin is talking to his little sister about monsters.

If a monster attacked us, I'd beat it up. If it had spikes I'd make it spike itself. I'd be so fast, he would just miss me and bang!

If the monster was slimy, I'd go to the fire station and spray water on him because probably if he wasn't slimy he would either die or maybe cheer up and not want to squash people.

I could too do it! I'm way stronger than you! Maybe if a monster attacked town the first thing I'd do is feed it my little sister. Monsters *love* to eat little sisters! They do, too, so you'd better watch it or maybe I won't save you!

ANNE

Anne is a girlie girl. She's talking to her friend who is a tomboy.

I don't like that doll. She's not pretty enough. I like dolls that look like ladies and wear high heels. When I'm older, I'll wear dresses and panty hose.

Your mom takes her panty hose off in the kitchen when she gets home? Ew! Well, *I* like pretty lady things. I'm going to have a hundred purses and five hundred shoes and a million dresses, all of them pink. And I'm going to wear *lots* of makeup. I will not look silly! I'll look beautiful. You'll be jealous.

LON

Lon went to the fire station on a school trip.
He wants to be a fireman.

Mom, can I have a string? We went to the firehouse today for a field trip, and the fireman said that if I bring a string to the station, I can pull a fire truck home. That's what he told me. So can I have a piece of string? If there's a fire, won't it be good to have a fire truck right outside? I could hold the hose with Dad while you run out of the house!

The fireman was not kidding. He meant it! He swore he'd give me the truck. Why can't I have some string, Mom?

JON PAUL

*Jon Paul lived in Africa. He's telling his friend
a story about something he saw there (or
did he?).*

When we lived in Africa, there were these big, blue
caterpillars there, big as a tall man. Big as a giraffe.
And they liked to sing and tap dance. The caterpillars want to smoke and drive race cars, but they
have no hands, so they can't. This makes them sad.
That's why they sing and dance. To cheer up.

They like to eat girls, too. There was this one cater-
pillar I knew named Charlie, and one day I saw him,
and he had this big lump in his belly. I said to him,
"What's that, Charlie? Did you eat a little girl?" He
nodded his head and burped and out slid this little
girl who was covered in yellow goo. So don't go to
Africa or blue caterpillars will eat you!

It is, too, true!

LUKE

Luke is reporting to Earth from his spaceship on Mars.

Captain O'Hara reporting from Mars. We just discovered Martians. They are all skinny and green. Plus, they smell weird. They smell like brussels sprouts. That's what everybody eats here: brussels sprouts! We have to leave this planet right away. They have never even heard of pizza. I tried to make them eat potato chips, but they said they were too stinky and crunchy. These Martians are crazy! Permission to fly back to Earth, sir!

JUSTIN

Justin thinks his dad is a spy and people are following him. He's telling his friend some tips about spies.

Not so loud! There are spies everywhere. See that guy over there in the big coat? He's a spy. My dad is a spy, too. But not a bad spy; he's an American spy. So we have to watch out for bad spies following us.

All guys with mustaches and big coats are spies. And ladies who are sexy are spies, too. Don't you watch the movies? It's a fact. Everybody knows that. So just be on the lookout and don't talk too loud. You never know who's listening!

FRANK

Frank is telling his friend what he wants to be like when he grows up.

When I get older, I'm going to get one hundred tattoos. I don't care if it hurts and they don't wash off. I'm going to get a hundred. I'm going to get a battleship and a skull—a whole bunch of stuff. It's going to look cool. They're going to be all over my arms. And then I'll wear short-sleeve shirts so everyone can see them.

I'm going to drive a motorcycle and a race car, too. And I'm going to own a pizza place. I'm never going to get a wife because they don't like to watch football on the weekends. Plus, girls are yucky. I am going to be the coolest guy in the entire world!

MILES

Miles is asking his mother for sneakers that light up when you walk.

Can I get the sneakers that light up when you walk? All the other kids have them. Every time you take a step there's this red light that flashes on the bottom. They are awesome. If I got those I would just look at my feet all day. I'd be so happy. I know my birthday isn't for a long time, but I've been really good. I think I deserve them. I cleaned my room last week, and I didn't complain.

I didn't stuff everything under the bed! I put them away right. So can I have them? I promise when my birthday comes, I won't ask for anything. Or at least not much. Can I, Mom? Can I?

TRAVIS

Travis has to go to the bathroom! He's talking to his teacher.

Please, Miss Martin? I know there's only five minutes left, but I need to go *now*. It's important. Really, really, really. I'm not lying. I can't wait. I really can't. Trust me. I'll run back to the classroom as fast as I can! OK, I won't run. I'll walk. But please let me go? Or else there will be a big mess in here. Please? I think I can't wait any—

I can? I can? Thank you! Thank you!

JENNA

Jenna's parents just got a divorce. Today was her first day at a new school in a new town.

I don't like my new teacher. I don't like my new school. I'm not going back. I hate it here. Let's go back home. Please? I hate this new place. I don't even get my own room anymore. Can't we move back with Dad? He'd let us. I know he would.

Why did we have to move? Everyone is mean here. No one talks to me. It's not fair. I want to go home, Mom.

ZORK

Zork is a robot. Or is he just a kid trying to get his room cleaned?

I am a robot. I am going to take over this whole world. I have all the power in the universe. You will do as I say. Clean my room! Make the bed! Do the dishes! Take me to the movies! If you don't, I will vaporize you with my eyes!

I am, too, a robot! Silence! Fine! I will make my demands more polite. *Please* clean my room. *Please* make the bed. *Please* do the dishes. *Please* take me to the movies. Or I will vaporize you!

Is that better?

JOSIE

Josie wants to be a Broadway star.

When I grow up, I want to sing. I'm going to be on Broadway. The lights are going to come on, and everyone will stare at me. I'll sing and dance and be sooooo good. Everyone will clap and scream and stand up—I'll be the most famous person in the world! I'll be *that* good. People will stand in line to buy tickets to see me. My hand will be tired all the time from signing autographs. I'll see pink and orange spots in front of my eyes from people taking pictures. I'll be the best singer in the whole world! You wait and see.

SUNNY

Sunny can see fairies. She tells her best friend all about it.

I saw a fairy today. Her name is Bella Bee. She's pretty with long, red hair all the way to her feet. She has white wings. She sits on my ear and tells me stories about happy things. She knows a little mouse named Gus who wears purple overalls with orange spots. He lives in the country. He's very silly. Some of the other mice don't like his clothes, but he doesn't care. Bella Bee and Gus go to the river and swim and tell jokes. Next time they go, I'm going with them. We are going to eat tiny cupcakes with pink icing. You can come, too, if you want. Just don't tell anyone else. It will be our secret!

Families!

You can't live with them;
you can't live without them.

ALISON

Alison is the oldest in her family.

I can tell you what to do if I want! I'm the oldest. That's the rule. You don't know anything because you're too little. I know a lot more than you. You're not even in school yet. School is very hard. Probably too hard for you. Now sit down and listen to me. I'll tell you what to do, and you'll be smarter.

Hey, where are you going? I'm trying to help you!

EMMETT

Emmett has a bossy older sister.

You think just because you're older you know every-thing. But you don't. You don't know anything. You've just been on Earth longer. That doesn't give you brains. Old people are not smarter or wiser. I bet there are a lot of dumb grandpas in the world. I bet there are grandpas so dumb that they can't fig-ure out how to work a rocking chair. They just sit there thinking, "How does this thing work?" That's what you're going to be like when you're old.

When I'm old I'm going to cure all the diseases in the world and be the president. So you'd better be nice to me, and stop bossing me around, dumb head.

LILLY

*Lilly wants to hang out with her older sister.
Her older sister, Jamie, wants Lilly to leave
her alone.*

I am *not* a baby! I'm as grown up as you. Why can't
I play with you and your friends? I'm as fast as you.
I can keep up. I can think of fun things to do. Like
why don't we bury the piggy bank in the backyard
so no one can steal it? That would, too, be fun!
What are you going to do that's so grown up? All
you and your friends ever do is sit around and talk
about boys. It's boring. I don't want to play with
Mom, Jamie; I want to play with you!

JASON

Jason is a sports fan. He's talking to his little brother, Eric.

What are you doing with that? I wanted that T-shirt. I've wanted it forever. So how come you got it? It's not fair. I liked the Eagles first. I did! I was *alive* first. I never get anything I want. Mom and Dad like you best 'cause you're the baby. Nobody likes me 'cause I'm old. It's so unfair! It's not my fault I was born first. How come every time I say I like something, Eric, you get it first? How come you always have to like what I like? You need to get your own personality and stop being so cute. And don't look at my Hanukkah list!

SARAH

Sarah's brother cut up her school uniform.

Guess what. Your trick didn't work. I bet you thought if you cut up my uniform, I'd go to school and everyone would see my underwear, and it would be funny. But guess what? I saw the hole you cut in my uniform *before* I put it on. I told Mom. So you're in trouble. Guess what else? I don't have to wear a uniform the *whole* rest of the school year because you ruined it. So, ha-ha. I get to wear regular clothes. So there!

ALEX

Alex can't find the money he was saving. He thinks his brother and sisters took it.

Where's my allowance? Somebody stole it! You must have. I didn't spend it. I've been saving forever. Every single quarter from Grandma and Grandpa. It's taken me ages to save up! And now it's gone. Somebody stole it. It wasn't a robber since the TV is still here. It must have been someone IN THIS HOUSE!

Oh yeah. I did buy that game last week. Never mind. Whoops.

LAURA

Laura wants to go look at herself in the mirror. She loves to look at herself!

Excuse me . . . I have to go look in the mirror. Well . . . I have to look because . . . I *like* to look at myself. I'm kind of cute when I'm sad. It makes me happy to see what I look like. Then I'm not sad anymore.

It does too make sense! It makes sense to *me*. Don't laugh, Debbie! I can't help it if I'm cute. Now you made me sad again so I *really* have to look in the mirror. Excuse me.

TOM

Tom is walking to school with his twin sister, who talks a lot.

Leave me alone. I just don't want to talk to you today. All you do is talk, talk, talk all morning. I need to think. I don't feel like talking. Or listening! Jeez, I'm not being mean, I'm telling the truth. I just like quiet. I like hearing the birds chirping and the wind blowing. I like stepping on leaves and looking at the sky.

OK—you asked for it. Your voice is too loud and annoying. Good! Go away! That's what I wanted in the first place!

SIMON

Simon has been spying on his family.

So, I called the whole family here for a reason. You're all in trouble. I've been paying attention to stuff lately. There's been a lot of rule breaking. Dad, you were cursing yesterday in the garage when you hurt your hand. You tell me never, ever to curse. Carol, you were picking your nose while you were watching TV. You always say it's gross when I pick my nose! Mom, you put onions in the soup, and you told Dad you didn't. That's a *lie*.

It is not wrong to tattle! Besides, you taught me to always tell the truth. I'm the best person in this whole family! So none of you can tell me what to do anymore.

CHARLIE

Charlie is very dirty from playing outside. His mom wants him to take his pants off before coming inside the clean house.

What was I doing today? Me and the guys were just messing around. We got these tree branches and were trying to hit each other with them. And then we were trying to learn how to slide into base. I guess we got a little dirty.

Mom, I can't take my pants off on the porch! People will see me! Can't I just come in the house? I'm not *that* dirty. I'll be *very* careful. There are a lot of parts of me that don't have any mud on them at all. Like my elbows. *(Looks at his elbows.)* OK, not my elbows. But, Mom, there are people walking by! You can't make me do this!

LEXIE

Lexie is trying to teacher her brother how to cross the street without getting hurt.

You have to look before you cross the street. *All* the time. You cannot *hear* the cars. You'll get killed. They could come out of nowhere, or the cars could be driving really fast. You need to be careful. Rules are there for a reason. I do not sound like Mom! Besides, Mom is smart. So maybe I do sound like Mom!

You sound like a dummy. Well, you're talking about doing dangerous things! It only takes a second or two to look before you cross the street, so just do it! Besides, if you don't, I'll tell Mom, and you'll get in trouble.

WALT

Walt doesn't want to go to the movies with his older sister, Marie. He's asking his mom to let him stay home.

No. I never want to go to the movies again! Not after the last time I went with Marie and her friends. They like to see scary movies. They won't ever see what I want.

Don't make me go! I'll stay at home. I'm old enough to take care of myself. I don't mind being all alone in the house at night . . . Actually, I guess I'll go to the movies, now that I think about it. Can you just tell Marie not to take me to a really scary one?

LEE

Lee's dad is watching the news. Lee wants to watch cartoons instead.

Why do you watch the news every night, Dad? It's booooooooring. It's always the same. The news is just a bunch of guys talking. It's JUST SO BORING! Can't we watch the cartoon channel? Don't you like to laugh? I feel like my head is going to explode all over this room I'm so bored—Pow! Splat! Smush!

Here, I'll be the news guy: "Tonight everyone is very boring in the whole world. The whole world is boring and bunch of other guys said boring things and the weather is boring. Have a boring night. I'm boring. Good night." That's it! I just did the news for you. Now you don't have to watch it! Let's watch cartoons!

ROB

Rob doesn't want to go to bed yet. His mom and dad want him to go to bed now.

I'm not tired. Why do I have to go to bed now? I'm wide-awake. I won't be tired in school. I just want to see the end of this show. Then I'll go to bed. It's over at eleven. You can't turn it off now! It's not over! I'll never know what happens now. This isn't fair. I never get my way. I always have to do what you say. It stinks being a kid. I can't wait till I'm a grown-up, and I can tell other people what to do. I'll stay up all night if I want! Then I'll tell *you* when to go to bed. Aw, fine. I'm going to bed now. I can't wait till I'm sixteen!

DOUG

Doug's mom just had a baby. He's not happy about it.

I have a new sister. She's a baby. She can't do anything by herself. It's annoying. She can't play, she can't feed herself, she can't walk. It's no fun. And my mom and dad run around for the baby all the time. Oh, man, can that baby cry! It's the loudest cry I ever heard. My mom is always saying to me, "Use your *inside* voice!" Well, this baby is not using her inside voice! And my mom never gets mad at her! When her diaper is dirty, man, it is stinky! I don't understand why anyone would want a baby. They're just not fun.

LINDSEY

Lindsey's mom just had a baby. She's very happy about having a new sister.

I have a new sister! She's all pink and cuddly and cute! Her face is all smushed up and she has the tiniest hands and feet I ever saw in my whole life. My dad says she looks like me. She's just got a little bit of fuzz on her head like a baby chick. I love to rub it. And sometimes I even get to hold her if I am very, very careful. You have to hold their head up or they fall down. When the baby is hungry, she looks like a baby bird with her mouth open. It's sooooo cute. I wish I had a baby. They are the cutest things in the whole world!

ALICE

Alice just had a nightmare. She wants to come into her mom and dad's room.

Mom? Can I come in? I just had a nightmare. I dreamed there was a monster with big, pointy teeth chasing me, and it could run at superfast speeds. And it came up to me and tried to eat my head off! I'm scared. Can I come sleep in your bed? I think the monster might come get me if I go back in my room. It can climb the tree and get in my window! I don't want to go back in there. Please? I promise I won't kick in my sleep this time. You won't even know I'm there. Just don't make me go back to my room tonight!

Thank you; thank you! You're the best mom ever!

SHONDA

Shonda wants to help her mom bake in the kitchen. She wants to be a chef when she grows up.

Mom, can I help? Why not? I'm good at baking. I do not make a mess! I do a good job. Can we make cookies? Chocolate chip? Everybody likes cookies.

I'm done with my homework. So I can help you. Please? I want to be Rachel Ray when I grow up. Can I use the rolling pin? I like the rolling pin.

You *want* me to watch TV? I *never* get to help. You told me you'd teach me to cook when I'm older, and I'm older now. I *know* you told me that last week, so I'm a whole week older now. I just want to help, Mommy!

Food Fights!

The good, the bad, and the yucky!

DANNY

Danny doesn't want to eat the healthy dinner his mother made.

Can we get pizza tonight? Please? I don't like fish and spinach, Mom; you know that. I hate spinach. It tastes like slug soup. Yes, it does! Did you ever have slug soup, Mom? I don't want to be like Popeye. I don't need big muscles until I'm twenty. Can you imagine what I'd look like with big muscles? Crazy! My clothes wouldn't fit me. I'd bust right out of them. So spinach and fish are not a good idea. I can have my coat on in two seconds, Mom. Seriously. Two seconds. You can order fish and spinach pizza if you like that slug soup so much.

HANNAH

Hannah hates broccoli. She is talking to her parents.

I hate broccoli. Why can't it taste good? Why can't food that's good for you taste good? Not even chocolate would make this taste better. How come scientists can do all kinds of great things, but they can't make broccoli taste good? Scientists should really work on it. This is important. Especially if all this stuff about it being healthy is true. But maybe it's a lie! Maybe some evil person just *wants* us to think it's good for you. Maybe it's bad. Maybe it's really bad! Maybe this broccoli will kill me! Maybe I'm allergic to it. I don't think it's safe, Mom. I think it's dangerous. Please don't make me. You can't make me! I won't do it! Broccoli is evil!

ADDY

Addy fell asleep while chewing gum. Now it's stuck in her hair!

(Screams.) Look what happened! Oh no, oh no, oh noooooo! What am I going to do? It won't come out!

No, Mom, you can't cut my hair! There must be another way! This is all Daddy's fault. He gave me that Hubba Bubba gum. Two whole pieces! I can't help that I fell asleep.

My hair will be way too short if you cut it! Can't you wash it out? Isn't there anything we can do? I don't want to lose all my hair!

DEREK

Derek is always hungry. He ate his lunch before coming to school, now he wants to eat his friend's lunch.

Mel, I don't have any lunch money! Can I borrow some? I do not ask all the time! I never ask. Come on, you always have lots of money.

OK, OK, I ate my lunch on the way to school again. I can't help it! I'm always hungry.

Buy a snack and milk, and we'll share them. Sharing is good! Don't you listen in class? That's what the teacher says. Do you want me to starve to death?

CASEY

Casey's family is poor. She doesn't have anything to eat for lunch. She doesn't want anyone to know she's poor.

Well, my mom is really busy. She was busy this morning doing a lot of stuff and . . . I don't have my lunch. Actually, I just forgot it. My mom made it, but I forgot it. I know I forgot it yesterday, too. My mom keeps forgetting to remind me; that's all. It's not her fault. I just forget stuff a lot.

My mom made me a peanut butter and jelly sandwich with strawberry jelly because she knows it's my favorite. No, I don't want any of your sandwich. I'm not hungry anymore. I'll just eat the sandwich my mother made me when I get home.

ZACK

Zack's stomach is growling very loudly, and it's not lunchtime yet. He's asking his teacher to let him eat before lunch.

I'm sorry. That was my stomach. I'm hungry. Is it lunchtime yet? I'm really hungry. I didn't like my breakfast, the cereal got soggy. Can I just get my lunchbox now? I'll just eat a little bit. Just a few bites? I'm just so hungry. Is it almost lunchtime? Ten o'clock? In the *morning*? It's only ten o'clock? Mr. Bell, I don't think I can wait until lunch. I think I might die. I'm not kidding. Can I please just have a bite of my sandwich? I'll do it quick so no one will see me. Please?

LOUIS

Louis is a picky eater. He only eats hot dogs.
He's over at his friend Jack's house, and
Jack's mom, Mrs. Jones, doesn't have any hot
dogs.

No, I'm sorry, Mrs. Jones, I don't eat that. I only eat hot dogs. You don't have hot dogs? Oh. Well, maybe I should go home then. That's all I eat. Hot dogs for breakfast, lunch, and dinner. Sometimes I eat two or three instead of just one. My mom says I'll grow out of it someday. I doubt it. I *love* hot dogs.

My little sister is worse. She only eats chicken soup. She sticks her pigtails in the soup and sucks it out of her hair. It's disgusting.

Well, tell Jack I'll see him later. I've got to go home and have a few hot dogs. I think it's a three-hot-dog day. See you later, Mrs. Jones!

MACK

Mack is giving his friend tips about how to hide vegetables.

Sure, mashed potatoes are good. But you can't eat them! If you eat them, where will you hide your vegetables? The whole job of mashed potatoes is to hide things you don't want to eat. Mothers always are bugged when you don't eat green things on your plate like broccoli and string beans, but if you don't finish your mashed potatoes, they don't care. So you can hide the green stuff *under* the mashed potatoes! Mashed potatoes are like a fort for yucky vegetables. You hide them inside and no one knows they're there. So you never get in trouble. Get it?

EMMA

It's dinnertime, and Emma's not hungry.

I'm not hungry anymore, Mom. I didn't eat before dinner. I just had some bread. A few slices. Seven. But that has nothing to do with it. I'm just not hungry anymore. Can I play video games now? Mom, I can't fit anymore in my stomach. It's not fair. I guess I'll be sitting here the rest of my life now. I'll just get old, and I'll never go to school. I'll just be really stupid and old because I'm not hungry. Is that what you want? Fine! I'll eat two bites of this, but don't be surprised if I throw up.

MEGAN

Megan likes to put ketchup on ALL of her food. Her friend is grossed out!

What? This is not gross. Ketchup makes everything taste better! I'm serious. Try it! The more ketchup, the better. My mom lets me have as much ketchup I want. I put it on everything—corn, carrots, chicken—everything! It's made with tomatoes, so it's good for you. But it doesn't taste like tomatoes, so it tastes good. So if I want to put ketchup on this salad, I will! Mmm-mmmm! Cucumbers with ketchup are awesome! This is going to taste *good*.

Double Trouble

School + Friends = Double Trouble!

SASHA

Sasha is arguing with her friend about who is shorter.

No way are you taller than me! I'm definitely a little bit taller than you. Come on; let's stand back to back. Ashley, who's taller?

No way! I'm taller. You're lying. Why would you say that? I thought we were friends. I don't want to be the smallest person in the class. When am I going to grow? There are four-year-olds taller than me. I can't stand it. I want to grow now! Now! *(Closes her eyes tight and concentrates so hard that she looks like she's in pain.)* Am I taller now? No? I'm doomed!

JILL

A girl in Jill's class is making fun of her because she has holes in her socks.

I don't know why I have holes in my socks. I just do. I mean, my mom buys me socks. Lots of times. All the time. I just don't want to ruin the nice ones by wearing them to school. I just wear those ones to church.

Sure my mom washes my clothes! I just . . . I just go and play before school and get dirty. It's no big deal. Who cares? I'd rather have fun than look perfect like Karen. She never runs or jumps rope. That's no fun at all. I'd rather be me. Who cares about socks anyway?

DANIELLE

It's picture day and Danielle's hair is a mess.
She's talking to the man taking the pictures.

It's picture day? How come no one told me? I didn't hear about it. Did you? Does everyone know about this except me?

Hey—how come you're taking our pictures after recess? This is double bad. My hair's all messed up now. I'm going to look crazy. And my mom's going to be mad.

Of course I don't have a brush! Who walks around with a brush? I'm in elementary school. I don't carry a purse. I'm just a little girl!

ISABELLE

It's picture day. Isabelle hates getting her picture taken!

I don't want to smile. I don't feel like it. I don't like getting my picture taken. I won't say cheese. I don't like cheese. I'm allergic. It makes me itchy and then I can't breathe. So cheese doesn't make me want to smile.

Why can't I just get my picture take like this? Please stop calling me cupcake, sir. I'm not a cupcake. I'm a girl.

Of course I don't have a boyfriend. You ask strange questions. I'm six. Why would I have a boyfriend? I don't even like boys. Can't you just take the picture?

Fine. Let's get this over with. *(Shows her teeth in a phony smile.)*

MARY JANE

Mary Jane goes to a Catholic school. She used to want to be a nun, but now she's not so sure.

Sister, I really like your dresses you wear and the thing on your head, but I don't think I'm good enough to be a nun. I think I kind of like being bad sometimes, like when my little brother gets annoying, or sometimes I even steal stuff from my older sister only it's not stealing 'cause I give it back and it's not THAT bad 'cause it's only lipsticks and things like that. So am I going to hell? 'Cause it seemed bad in that movie we watched. But there was one part I didn't get. There was that picture of how hell was so bad 'cause they couldn't use their arms to eat, even though there was loads of food piled in front of them. I just kept thinking, why don't they just put their face in their food, like pigs?

Oh, that was a bad thing to say. I can tell. I'm never going to be a nun, am I?

ELLIE

Ellie's always getting chased and kissed by the boys. She's on the playground talking to her friends.

Why do boys have to chase me all the time? I'm so tired of running. I don't want to be kissed! Why can't boys be nice and normal?

Well, of course I want to have babies. So? You do not have to kiss a boy for that! You just get married, that's all. OK, maybe you kiss the boy once when you are at the church real quick, but that's it! Maybe I'll be in the Olympics instead. After all, I am faster than Bobby McGee, and everybody thinks he's the fastest kid in the class. But he hasn't kissed me yet!

MADDY

Maddy is talking to her friend about her report card.

What does S mean? I got an S in Social Studies.
What? That means I'm just OK? I'm better than OK,
though. I'm great! What means great? An O?
Well, why didn't I get O's? Did you get any O's?
You got *all* O's? That's not fair! I'm as good as you
are. You're Miss Lowly's favorite. It's not fair. I
don't see how you're better than me.

I'm not saying you're bad, Suzy. I'm just saying I'm
as good as you are. I just forget to do my homework
sometimes. But I'm still as smart as you!

LUCY

Lucy is afraid of stepping on a crack and breaking her mother's back. She's walking to school with her friend, Rachel.

Rachel! Look where you're going! And slow down, for Pete's sake. I can't go faster. I've got to keep from stepping on the cracks in the sidewalk.

How do *you* know that it won't break my mother's back? What if it does? My older sister broke a mirror once, and she's had bad luck ever since. She had to do third grade twice and her best friend in fifth grade doesn't like her anymore.

Which is worse: being late for school or breaking your mother's back? So let's slow down, Rachel, before someone gets seriously hurt.

GRANT

Grant is worried about his friend walking on railroad tracks.

Don't walk on the railroad tracks! You'll get killed. You can too get hurt or killed. My brother told me so. It's true. He knows a guy who got flattened. He looked like a pancake.

You don't care if a train runs over you? Fine, then just keep walking on the train tracks then. See if I care.

Stop kidding around! You're not funny.

LIA

Lia is lost with her friend, Becca. She's getting scared.

Where are we? I don't recognize anything. It looks like it's going to rain. I'm scared, Becca. What if we can't find our way home? I've never come this far before. We can't get in a car with a stranger!

No! You can't ask anyone for directions. They're *strangers*. You're not supposed to talk to strangers. We just have to keep walking. Don't cry. We have to be brave. We'll find the way home somehow.

NELL

Nell is having a hard time learning to read.

I don't like books. I don't like reading. It's hard. I don't know why it's so important. Who cares what happens in a crummy old book? I can just watch TV instead.

I don't care about reading menus and signs. I know what a stop sign looks like. And I'll order grilled cheese all the time. So I don't need to read.

It will take a lot less time in school! I can just do gym class and math. If I really need something read to me, I'll ask my mom. I think this is a great idea! School would be a lot more fun without reading.

WILL

Will isn't very good at math. His math teacher is not being nice to him, so he's hiding in the bathroom during math class.

I'm never coming out. Don't tell. I'm just going to stay in here. I hate this class. I hate Mrs. Stupidhead. She's always mean to me. Don't tell, Mark? You can stay in here, too, if you want.

You're good at math. It's not fair. She made me do the same problem *six* times yesterday. She tells me I don't listen. I *do* listen! She's too mean. Please don't tell her where I am. You won't get in trouble. I'm just going to stay in the bathroom during math from now on, that's all. I'm never going back. I don't care what anyone says.

KELLY

Kelly is the teacher's pet. The teacher, Mrs. Banks, had to leave the classroom for a minute. As soon as Mrs. Banks left the room, all the kids went crazy.

Now Mrs. Banks left me in charge. Stop it, Martin! She said you were supposed to be good while she's gone! Don't throw paper airplanes. Hey! Don't throw anything. If a rubber band gets shot in someone's eye they could go blind. Stop it! Listen to me! I'm in charge.

Harper, don't talk! You're supposed to be doing math problems. Don't make fun of me. I'm telling, everybody! You're gonna be in trouble when the teacher gets back. Why isn't anyone listening to me?

IKE

Ike is in the mall with some friends. Ike is afraid of escalators.

I hate escalators. I think they could eat my pants if they got caught, and I'd end up with no leg or no pants, or maybe both! The escalator would be eating my leg and my mother would be screaming and trying to pull me out, and my pants would come off, and everybody would see me in my underwear and laugh. It would be awful. So I'm taking the stairs.

Maybe I am weird. But I am going to keep my legs and my pants on forever. I'm not taking any chances. See you later, alligator.

SONIA

Sonia's friend is drawing the same thing as her in art class.

You can't draw a rainbow. I'm drawing a rainbow. You can't copy. I drew one first. So you have to do something else. Do a sunshine with a little smiley face. I love them. They're so cute.

You don't like sunshines with smiley faces in them? That's weird. See? That's so cute. Except I can do a cuter one. I'll show you.

OK, fine. I won't do one *now* since you did one, but I'll show you next time. You can't do one next time, too! You don't own sunshines with smiley faces! I called it first!

MARISSA

Marissa likes to draw. She gets a good idea to make the walls of her house look better.

I don't like any of this wallpaper. It's too plain. I could make it pretty. I would make the walls have castles and animals. That would be pretty, right? I'll draw what I want to do. I bet Mommy will really like it. I'll make the dining room extra pretty. She'll be so happy when she gets home and sees it!

TIM

Tim is talking to a girl in his class with long, blond hair.

So how do you grow your hair so long? Boys' hair only grows short. How come it doesn't get stuck in things like car doors and fences and stuff? Do you sit on it? I don't know why you'd keep it like that. Girls with long hair fall down when you push them. It's a fact! Your hair is too heavy. Your hair is really yellow, too.

Blond and yellow are the same thing! What are you getting so mad for? I'm just saying your hair is weird. That's all. Jeez, take it easy.

JED

Jed just pulled a girl's hair. She's crying.

Why are you crying? I didn't hurt you. I barely touched you. Stop being a baby. Don't call the teacher. I didn't mean to pull your hair. OK, I did, but I didn't mean to hurt you. You just have such a big ponytail. I had to pull it. I couldn't stop myself. I'm sorry, OK?

Yeah, we can be friends. No, I don't want to marry you! Why are you crying *now*?

MO

Mo is talking to his Uncle Henry about school.

I'm not six. I'm six and four months. So I'm older than a lot of kids at school. And I'm also taller than a lot of kids in my class. I won a race last week in gym class. There's this kid in my class, Ben, and he wins a lot, but I beat him last Wednesday. I'm going to beat him all the time now. I'm going to be the best runner in the class. I practice at home. Mom says I'm so fast she can't even see me sometimes. I'm like a blur. So, yeah, school is pretty good, Uncle Henry. I like it.

KATY

Katy is making fun of a girl in her class, Darla, by repeating everything she says.

"Stop repeating everything I say!" "I said stop it!" "Quit it!" "You're going to get in trouble if you don't stop!" "I'm telling!" "That's it! I'm going to the teacher."

Wait! Darla, I was just kidding! Can't you take a joke? How come you have to be so serious all the time? You're always running to the teacher. Learn to take a joke. Jeez! Hey, stop repeating me! I said stop it! It's not funny. I did this already! You're not original. Quit it!

NINA

Nina just found out from her best friend, Ashley, that she wasn't invited to their friend Britney's sleepover party.

Britney is having a party? Tonight? Oh. I guess . . . I didn't get invited. Maybe she forgot? Or it got lost? I thought we were friends. Did everybody else get invited? That's so mean! I was never, ever mean to *her*.

I don't like Britney! I don't care that I'm not going to a party. She's not my friend anymore. Why don't you come over to my house instead of going to her party?

If you go to her party, you won't be my friend anymore, Ashley. I won't be friends with you, either.

EVE

*Eve just got caught daydreaming by her
teacher. She's talking to her friend.*

I hate it when Mrs. Baker yells at me. I try so hard
to be good. I do everything she says most of the
time. I just was thinking about something for a second and forgot to pay attention. I was thinking
about what it would be like to live in the White
House. I don't know why she gets so mad. I didn't
do it on purpose. I used to like her at the beginning
of the year, but now I don't. She didn't have to yell
at me in front of everybody. I want to go home.

ADAM

Adam is arguing with his best friend over what is the best number.

You like the number one? That's so obvious. My favorite number is eight. I don't know why, it's just the best one. Even numbers are better than odd ones. I mean, they're called odd numbers. They're weird. It's right in the name.

I can't wait until I'm eight. I think that will be the best year ever. When I'm eight, I'm going to have a huge party. My mom already told me I could. I'm going to have a piñata. I always wanted one. See? I told you eight is the best number.

OLIVIA

Olivia tells her best friend about her new favorite color.

I don't like pink anymore. Now I like red because cherries are red. I like cherries. They're so cute. I want a shirt I saw in a store with cherries. It's cute. My mom might buy it for me. You'll like it. What's your favorite color?

You like blue! Blue is a boy color. So is green! You can like yellow or purple if you want. I am not bossy! Stop telling me I'm bossy! I'm just telling the truth. I guess you can like light blue since it's the color of the sky.

CHRIS

Chris's friend, Peter, doesn't want to visit his house any more.

Mom, Peter won't come over. He says he's allergic to Butch. I think he's just scared 'cause last time Butch knocked him over and slobbered all over him. Butch is just being friendly; I tried to tell him!

Or maybe Peter won't come 'cause he got stung by a bee and swelled up like a watermelon. I don't know. I don't know why Peter won't come. We had such a good time last time he was over! He even got stitches! I always wanted stitches. Good things never happen to me!

WENDY

Wendy put her clothes on by herself this morning. But she didn't pay enough attention.

What? My pants are backwards? No, they're not. Oh, you're right! What can I do? I can't take them off right here on the playground! If I just stand here behind this tree, maybe no one will see me. Oh, no! The fire alarm! Now everyone will see me. Billy will make fun of me. No one will be my friend. I will never, ever be the President of the United States and an artist now. I'm doomed! Why did this have to happen to me?

ALISHA

Alisha thinks she can win any fight. Here, she tells her friend why.

"Mind your own beeswax!"

I am really good at arguing. I always win. I know just what to say. "I know you are, but what am I?" No one can say anything after that. My brother is a big pain, and I say that to him a lot. It makes him go away. Here's one I just made up, "Your head is full of mud holes!"

Who cares if it makes sense? It's not stupid! Your head is full of mud holes! It is, too! Make like a bee and buzz off, Kiki.

See, I won! I always win!

FRANCIS

*Francis is afraid of snakes. He doesn't want
to go on the class trip to the zoo.*

Do I have to go to the class trip? I don't want to. I
don't like the zoo. This one kid in the class told me
there are snakes there. I don't like snakes. I like bears
and penguins, but if they make me see snakes . . .
I don't know. I just don't want to go. Can't I stay
home that day? Can't you just skip work that day
and stay home with me? What if all the other kids
like snakes? What if the snakes get out?

Maybe you could call the teacher and ask her if we
can only see animals. If she promises we won't see
anything scary, I guess I'll go.

Lucky/Unlucky

There are good days, and
there are not so good days!

TAMARA

Tamara is telling her friend about going on a hot-air balloon ride.

Once I went up in a hot-air balloon. It was blue and red and yellow and orange stripes. Everyone waved at us when we went up in the sky. We went so high that people were like specks. We flew over the tops of trees. It looked like I could walk on the tops of them. The sky was so blue. And the balloon made a loud whooooooosh sound that made me hold my ears. You put hot air in the balloon to go up high. And we landed in a little field and people ran out to clap for us. That was the most fun I ever had in my life. I can't wait till I get to do it again!

STEVEN

*Steven has been out of school all week. He
tells his friend why.*

I've had a bad week. Sure, I was out of school, but
still, I did not have a good week. First I had to go to
see my grandma, and she thinks I'm three years old.
She makes a lot of stew. I hate stew. And she pinches
my cheeks and says I'm cute. I have to be polite all
the time and smile. It made my face hurt. Then I
came home and my goldfish, Alfred, died. It was
floating on the top of the fish tank. Then, worst of
all, I got a dime stuck in my nose. I had to go to the
hospital. It was gross. I hope this week is better. It
has to be!

JENNIFER

Jennifer just got a new kitten. Last night she played with it all night, but this morning she can't get out of bed. The kitten keeps grabbing at her feet every time her feet touch the ground. She calls her dad for help.

Help! Daddy! Help me! I thought the new kitty was my friend, but now he's trying to kill me! Every time I try to get out of bed, he goes to grab my feet with his claws! I'm scared. I don't like the kitten anymore. We were playing yesterday, how come he doesn't like me today?

This is how he plays? He *likes* me? He should just purr and be sweet. That's what kitties are supposed to do. Maybe I'll like him again later, but for now, can you just take him out of my room so I can go to the bathroom?

SAM

Sam just opened a Christmas present that he doesn't like.

What is this for? Is this a joke? 'Cause it's not funny. Does Santa think I'm a girl? This is a girl's present! I never asked for a little horse for Christmas. Is Santa some kind of joker?

No, I'm not giving it to you, Sarah. I don't care if you want it. Unless you've got a trade! I am not getting less presents than you.

No way! I don't want that stupid doll. This isn't fair! Wait—you got an army tank. I want that! You can't keep it, that's mine! You don't like it. You're lying to me. That's my tank and this is your stupid horse.

Mom! Sarah's stealing my tank truck from Santa!

OLIVER

Oliver likes to try new things. Today, he tried something new, and it didn't go very well.

Um, Mom? I made a little mistake. I sort of . . . the drain in the sink is all clogged up. I didn't do anything! It did it by itself. All I did was just drop something in there by accident. Well . . . it was . . . my oatmeal. It just fell in and got jammed in the drain.

I don't know how! It just happened! I'm sorry, Mom, it was an accident! I didn't do it on purpose. Well, maybe I did, but I didn't know it would clog the drain. Sorry, Mom.

PATRICK

*Christmas is coming, and Patrick hasn't been
a good boy all the time.*

Dad, remember when I crashed my Hot Wheels into
the wall in the living room and made that hole? Do
you think Santa will know about that?

He sees everything? Well, do you think it will make
him mad? Most of the time I've been really good
and nice. Don't you think so? I really want that
remote control car on my list. Do you think I'll get
it? What if I'm really good between now and
Christmas? I'll go clean my room right now! And I'll
be nice to Missy almost all of the time! I'm going to
be the best kid ever.

PETER

Peter just found out the tooth fairy gave his friend a lot more money than him.

The tooth fairy gave you five dollars? Five dollars?! I got a *quarter* for my last tooth. A lousy quarter!

What is going on here? Is there more than one tooth fairy? I'll never get a bike at this rate. I have to have about ten million teeth fall out to get that bike!

I think my tooth fairy needs to be fired. She stinks. I'm going to ask my dad tonight if we can move closer to your house. Maybe then I'll get the *good* tooth fairy!

T.J.

T.J. lives on a busy street. He is looking out the window with his friend, Brandon.

Do you see all those people outside my house? God makes them walk by. They have to. Just for me. That's what my mom told me. Every time I think, "Please, God, make someone walk by now," they do. It's 'cause I go to church on Sunday. Plus, I think I'm going to be the pope when I'm older, so I'm special.

Sure, you could try it, but it might not work for you. Go ahead; try it!

Well, OK. It worked that one time, but that's because *I* wanted that guy to walk by, too. If you tried it by yourself, it wouldn't work.

MATT

Matt got new cowboy boots for his birthday.
He wore them for the first time today.

Mom? Mom! Mom, I love my new cowboy boots.
They're awesome. Yeah, we walked to the store and
got slushies. I got a cherry cola one. But, Mom,
don't be mad at me. I love my cowboy boots,
but . . . they kind of hurt. I think maybe my feet are
kind of bleeding. It feels like my feet blew up, and I
don't think I can get them off. Are you mad at me?

Sorry. I really love them. Maybe next time I just
shouldn't wear them *all* day. Maybe I'll just wear
them half a day. Can you help me get them off?
Thanks, Mom.

EVAN

Evan is in the hospital for the first time ever.
He's talking to his mom.

How come there are no bathrooms in the hospital?
What do all the really sick people do when they
have to stay here a long time? There *are* bathrooms?
Where? Oh. Well . . . Mom, I think I did something
I wasn't supposed to do. See that plant in the hall? I
kind of thought it was the only place to go. Sorry.
Yeah, I just walked over to it. I was desperate,
Mom. I really had to go. Am I going to get in trou-
ble now? No one saw me!

OK. It will be our secret!

ABOUT THE AUTHOR

Kristen Dabrowski is an actress, writer, acting teacher, and director. She received her MFA from The Oxford School of Drama in Oxford, England. The actor's life has taken her all over the United States and England. Her other books, published by Smith and Kraus, include *The Ultimate Monologue Book for Middle School Actors Volume I: 111 One-Minute Monologues*, *The Ultimate Audition Book for Teens Volume III: 111 One-Minute Monologues*, *Twenty 10-Minute Plays for Teens Volume 1*, the *Teens Speak* series (four books), and the educational *10+* play series (six books). Currently, she lives in the world's smallest apartment in New York City. You can contact the author at monologuemadness@yahoo.com.